# Amma, Tell Me About

# Diwali !

Written by
Bhakti Mathur

Illustrated by
Mayashree Somani

It was as if the stars themselves
Came down to earth that night -
The entire city was lit up
With thousands and thousands of lights!

It was Diwali, the festival of lights,
That Klaka had celebrated today.
Oh, how much fun it all had been -
A most wonderful, beautiful day!

He'd woken up full of excitement
And worn new clothes with joy.
Amma and Daddy had spoilt Klaka so,
Giving many gifts to their little boy.

Friends, uncles, aunts and cousins streamed in
Through the day with good wishes and cheer.
In the evening, all the children had lit up the house
With rows of small earthen oil lamps, called diyas.

Then, together they offered their prayers
For good fortune, prosperity and health,
To Ganesha, the God of new beginnings
And to Lakshmi, the Goddess of wealth.

Ganesha has an elephant's head;
And on his feet, his pet mouse rests.
He brings good luck, clears obstacles,
And is worshipped before any quest.

Lakshmi, the Goddess of wealth,
Sits on a big lotus flower.
She has four hands to bless us with
And bestow fortune and power.

Then it was time for firecrackers
Sparklers making circles of light,
Wheels spinning wildly, rockets flying high,
Brightly burning flares - oh what a sight!

Finally it was time to sleep
But Klaka still chattered happily.
Climbing into bed, he said,
"Amma, tell me about Diwali!"

"Diwali takes its names from diyas," said Amma
"Just like the ones that you lit tonight.
It falls in autumn every year on 'amavasya',
The new moon day and the month's darkest night.

Diwali is also very special as it marks
For many Indians, the start of the new year.
A time to look ahead to new beginnings
And pray for fortune and good cheer."

"But why is Diwali named after diyas?"
Asked Klaka, ever as curious as can be.
"To answer that," said Amma and smiled,
"I have to tell you about Rama and his story..

Rama was the prince of Ayodhya,
Son of King Dasratha the Great.
He was brave and kind and loved by all,
Next in line to be King of the state.

But Kaikeyi, Rama's wicked stepmother,
Wanted her own son to be king instead.
She threw a big tantrum and demanded that
Rama be banished for fourteen years ahead.

Poor King Dasratha, was helpless,
For while he was sworn to do Kaikeyi's bidding,
How could he banish his beloved son Rama,
For fourteen years to a forest most forbidding?

But noble Rama knew what he had to do
He consoled Dasratha thus while wiping his tears:
"To uphold a promise made by my great father,
Gladly, will I go to the forest for fourteen years."

Taking off his crown, Rama left the kingdom at once
With wife, Sita and brother Lakshmana, by his side.
All of Ayodhaya came out to bid them farewell,
There was not one person there who wasn't teary-eyed!

The princes soon made the forest their home
And settled down happily in their new life.
Till Ravana, the ten-headed demon king of Lanka,
Hearing of Sita's beauty, decided to make her his wife.

Evil Ravana, kidnapped Sita from their home,
One day while Rama and Lakshmana were away.
Shocked to find Sita gone upon their return,
The princes looked everywhere in utter dismay.

Their search brought them to Kishkindha,
Where they met the mighty Hanuman.
Saddened to hear of Sita's kidnapping,
He promised the help of his monkey clan.

And thus an army of mighty monkey warriors,
Was raised in support of Rama's quest.
Onwards they marched to Lanka unafraid:
Till Sita was rescued, they swore not to rest!

On reaching Lanka they faced the demon army
And fought a most fearsome war.
People say that such a great battle
Had never been fought before.

Finally, Rama and Ravana came face to face,
In a fight that was fierce and heated.
Rama emerged victorious in the end -
Evil Ravana and his army were defeated.

Sita was released and reunited with Rama,
The loving couple were together at last.
It was also the end of fourteen years and so
The term of Rama's banishment had passed.

Carrying the three on his mighty shoulders,
Hanuman flew to Ayodhya that very night.
As they neared the city they were guided,
By thousands of diyas, giving off a golden light!

You see, the people of Ayodhya had not forgotten
That the fourteen years of Rama's exile had passed.
And so they had lit up diyas across the entire city,
To welcome their Rama to Ayodhya at last!

Since then, on Diwali day we remember
Rama's homecoming by lighting diyas.
Celebrate the victory of good over evil
And Rama becoming the King of Ayodhya."

"What a wonderful story Amma," said Klaka,
"I will surely light many more diyas next year."
"Lighting more diyas alone will not do," said Amma
"As you will learn from this next story, my dear.

Goddess Lakshmi comes to earth
On this day of Diwali every year.
To bless Rama's true followers
With fortune, prosperity and cheer.

Now, Lakshmi's blessings can bring untold riches.

So, people got greedy - money was all they cared about.

To attract the Goddess to their house first

They used bright lights to make it stand out.

Year after year as Lakshmi visited earth on Diwali,
The lights in every house got more and more bright.
Till one year, the glare was so bad it hurt her eyes,
And so, Lakshmi decided to turn back for the night.

As she turned to leave, at a distance she saw
A flicker of light in a house, nothing more.
Curious, she reached the small cottage
And knocked; a lady appeared at the door.

The Goddess said "I am Lakshmi,
Long into the night I have progressed.
Tired of all the bright lights in the city,
I have come to your cottage, may I rest?"

The lady invited her in to relax;
The Goddess found her very kind.
Lakshmi said, "May I ask you a question?
Something has been on my mind.

While the whole city is glowing with lamps
To entice me to their homes tonight,
How come your little cottage
Only has the one small light?"

The lady said "Oh, I am a poor seamstress
And I only have this one light.
I was busy finishing my work
And did not realise it is Diwali night!"

Hearing this Lakshmi blessed her,
For she had met a true devotee
Who did not think of pleasing the Gods,
And instead, went and did her duty.

So Klaka, true happiness comes to those
Who are dedicated to their work.
Just praying and lighting diyas alone
Will not bring you fortune and luck.

So always work hard,

Give your best to what you do.

Honesty and dedication are the only diyas

That will guide Lakshmi to you."

# Books in the 'Amma Tell Me' Series:

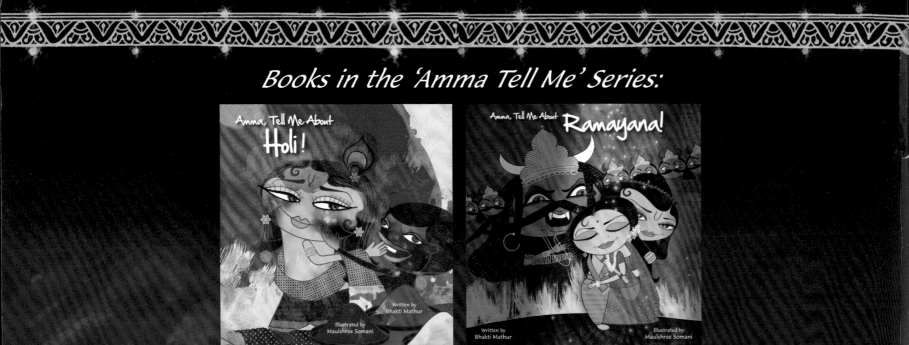